BeWILD

MUDDLED MAZE

...AGE

SLIPPERY SLOPE

FARTREE

WITCH'S HOUSE

First published in Great Britain
by Holly Day & Bump Publishing.

ISBN: 978-0-9555543-1-5

Seventh Edition

www.BeWILDerwood.co.uk

The Ballad of BeWILDerwood

A Boggle poem with lots of pictures

Tom Blofeld

Illustrated by Steve Pearce

Boating gently in the marshes, through the rushes and the reeds,
Here is Swampy, a marsh Boggle, finding food among the weeds.
He's off to catch some fish so his Mum can cook her pies,
Which are just completely yummy, and exactly the right size.

Swampy loves a pie or two (or three or four or five!)
It's not that he is greedy, he just likes to stay alive.
But mostly he is very good, and listens to his Mum.
They laugh together at his jokes whenever they feel glum.

(The very biggest Boggle only grows up to your knees
So going to their houses can be rather a tight squeeze.)

Swampy's Mum believes that it is better not to roam:
"Boggles shouldn't go too far. They're safer here at home."
As Swampy wasn't very brave he did what he was told,
But today was really lovely. He thought, "Maybe I'll be bold.
Perhaps I'll see the Scary Lake. I wonder if I dare.
No-one else I know at home has ever ventured there."

So off he went, much further than he'd ever been before.
He came across a massive lake, and pushed out from the shore.
"It's very **BIG**," he thought aloud. A gulp grew in his throat.
Then *SPLOOSH* and *SPLASH* and water jets exploded by the boat.

Boggles mostly go quite slow when travelling alone,
But they can be really zippy when they need to get back home.

No-one in the Village knew what had made the splash,
And everyone agreed that going back there would be rash.
Then Swampy thought about his friends who lived up in the wood.
His cousins, Moss and Leaflette, would help him if they could.

So Swampy went adventuring twice in just two days.
Anyone would think that he'd forgotten Boggle ways.
His friends were waiting for him, waving in the trees.
They lived there in a Twiggle house, high up in the leaves.
They didn't know what made the *SPLASH* but Leaflette said, "We should
Go and ask the friendly Witch who lives beyond the woods."

And so the happy trio set off that summer's day.
They danced along, singing songs they made up on the way.

Boggle Travelling Song

We're travelling today *(Tum Tumpty Tum),*
And singing on our way *(Hum Humpty Hum).*
There's a warm blue sky,
We've sweetsludge pie,
And all the world's Okay *(Way Hay Hay!)*

(Boggles sing noisily most of the time,
But they always sing LOUDEST on the last line.

Then everyone makes up other verses.
I wonder which one will invent the most worstest.)

The forest was filled with the chatter of birds.
  Then coming towards them the travellers heard
Groans, which were mixed with terrible thumps,
It frightened the Boggles and made them all jump.
Though Boggles aren't good at climbing up trees,
They zipped through the branches, scraping their knees.
  They peeked cautiously out of the leaves and the twigs
At a creature below that was noisy and big.
A huge leggy monster with spines on its back.
  Maybe Boggles were just what it liked for a snack?

But Leaflette was brave and she talked to the beast
 To find if it wanted a big Boggle feast.
She asked, "Are you a friend or are you a foe?"
The spider just smiled and said, "Not a foe, no."
 But if you are kind I'd like you to help,
This hole in my boot is making me yelp.
It's hard finding shoes when your legs number eight,
 So I don't mind what sort, except roller-skates!"

 "I am the Thornyclod spider," it said,
 And it showed them a foot without any tread.
So Swampy and Moss began to climb down,
Landing with great big *THUMPS* on the ground.
"Of course we will bring you a boot," called out Moss.
"A broken down shoe is a terrible loss!
We'll be back with the footwear later today.
 I'm sure that the Witch will show us the way."

(The Witch, you'll remember
was friendly and good,
Though she's fierce if you
don't behave as you should.)

They soon met the Witch
with her pet robin, Rosie.
She gave them some fruit
while the Boggles got cosy.
Then Swampy explained
how he'd been to the lake,
Where the terrible *SPLASH*
had made his knees quake.
The Witch wasn't sure
what had made Swampy wet
But she thought for a
while and then said, "I bet
I know of a person who'll tell you the truth.
He's explored every part of this place in his youth.
To get there you will all have to walk for a while,
But he'll know what it was." Said the Witch with a smile.
"And as for the Thornyclod's tickly toes;
Go to the tree, which instead of fruit, grows
All kinds of boots and slippers and shoes.
I'm sure you will find a good one to choose."

Can you **find the five purple shoes?**

There were lots of fun ways to get through the wood,
 But the best was a log that had split so you could
Slide all the way down it, whizzing along.
(Swampy went backwards but still found it fun!)
And if they felt lost there were signposts to read
Which pointed out for them the path that they'd need,
 But as they kept going, there were too many tracks,
So none of them thought they could find their way back.

 Then the signs became odder,
saying things like "Not Here,"
And "Probably Not," and
"The Wrong Way, I Fear."
"I think that we're lost,"
Leaflette said to her friends,
 "There are too many
signposts and too
 many bends."

Just as they feared they would never be found,
Moss spotted some footprints, there, on the ground.
"Let's follow these marks, they may lead us out."
Then Swampy was pointing. They all shouted out:
"It's the Thornyclod spider, and this is its lair
And there it is cooking some food over there."
It was waving a ladle, and then it began
To cook up some sticky sweet mess in a pan.
"I'm making marshmallows," it said to the three.
"With the very best marsh I can find, for my tea."

So they all tried a bit, and their chattering ceased.
It tasted quite good, but it glued up their teeth!
But they swallowed it down, eventually.
Then the Thornyclod waved its boot at a tree:
"Follow past there and you'll go the right route."
They thanked it profusely, and gave it a boot
Which fitted its foot, so the spider looked thrilled.
Then they travelled on humming a song Leaflette trilled.

Join in the fun and **find your way** into the **Thornyclod's Muddled Maze!!**

No way
Up there!
This way
That way

The butterflies were flying in a gentle summer breeze
As Moss, Leaflette, and Swampy journeyed gaily through the trees.
They rested in a shady spot to eat some sweetsludge pie,
Then they were in the Dark Woods, where you hardly see the sky.

But soon it was too difficult to tell which way to go.
Spiky bushes blocked the way and travelling was slow.
As the Boggles looked around at the beeches and pine,
They saw no way to carry on. Then Swampy saw a sign.

The sign was very old, and it was broken here and there.
It pointed to "The Broken Bridge," right up in the air.
And also, rather oddly, was something more as well:
"Be Bats," it read, but why it did, Swampy couldn't tell.

So they climbed up in the trees to find the bridge high in the sky.
They clambered through the branches, but then Leaflette gave a cry.
Right at the very top they found a dreadful thing to view:
A terrifying wobbly bridge – with the middle broken through.

The Boggles stood in silence wondering how to get across.
It looked too wide a gap to jump. Then they all heard Moss:
"That sign which read 'Be Bats,' that we all saw down below,
Should have said 'Beware of Bats,' but broke off long ago."

He pointed through the leaves at little black dots way up high,
A cloud of angry bats was circling, swarming in the sky.

They all had teeth. They looked so fierce, it didn't do to wait,
For they were coming closer now, and eyeing them like bait.

"Follow me!" called Swampy and he ran off with his pole.
He vaulted straight up in the air and right across the hole.
He put some planks across the gap, so the others could cross too,
And then they ran at lightning speed. They very nearly flew.

They made it to the other side, just in time to see,
The bats wheel off high in the sky, disappointedly.
"Wasn't Swampy really daring and very clever too?"
Said Leaflette smiling at the bravest Boggle that she knew.

Normally a Boggle finds that climbing down a tree
Means landing with a *BUMP*, after falling painfully.
But Leaflette found another way to travel to the ground:
She hooked a twig across a rope and slid the whole way down.
So on they travelled, through the woods, singing happy songs,
When Swampy's nose began to smell a lovely marshy pong.
"This is where the Witch said we'd find the help we need.
The Old Man In The Marshes should be somewhere in these reeds."

They met him in his muddy bath among the sedge and scrub.
He was looking for his loofah to give his back a rub.
All the Boggles saw of him was just his head and nose,
But he heard their tale of water jets, and then said, "I suppose
I could tell you, but I'd prefer you find out on your own,
Because on this great adventure I believe that you have grown
Into brave intrepid Boggles. So this is what to do:
Go through the marshes to the lake. The rest is up to you."

They were just about to follow down the route the Old Man said,
When Leaflette noticed something that was growing on his head.
He let her take a bunch of lovely flowers sprouting there
That the Witch had asked her for, as they were very rare.

(The Witch can help in lots of ways, but never ever tells
Just what goes in her potions or how to make her spells).

Not far into the marshes, the going got quite rough
 And Moss got all caught up in some spiky spiny stuff.
Leaflette went a different route, and Swampy found that he
Was all alone, as he plunged on, through bushes, reeds and trees.

   The next thing he knew he had reached the lakeside edge.
He listened: there was something noisy lurking in the sedge.
Then *whoosh*, and he was soaking from a massive water burst.
 He plunged back in the bushes and he waited for the worst.
Swampy shivered, as he hoped that Boggles didn't feature
 On the menu of the thing out there, a great green swishy creature.

"Hello!" It shouted, waving, with all its teeth in sight,
But smiling in a friendly way. Perhaps it wouldn't bite?
"I'm Mildred," said the creature. "Will you be friends with me?
   I try so hard to make new friends but people mostly flee.
I only eat green vegetables and fruit when they are sweet.
But perhaps a spiny Crocklebog is frightening to meet.'

Swampy smiling cautiously, said, "I'll be friends with you."
If you promise not to make that *SPLASH* and soak me when you do.
   It makes me very nervous and it's not good for my health."
"I'm really sorry," Mildred said. "I just forget myself."
 You see, when I'm all excited I forget to breath the air,
So out comes lots of water, but it isn't meant to scare."

So Swampy and the Crocklebog talked happily of food.
They both agreed that Sweetsludge pie and Barkicrisps were good.
"Why don't you come and meet my friends?" said Swampy to the Beast.
"We could cross the lake together, then all have a scrumptious feast."
So Swampy hopped on Mildred's back (a little carefully),
And soon all four·were swishing off, across the shiny sea.

Swampy's Mum was very pleased the travellers had returned.
The villagers all gathered round to hear what he had learned.
When the three had told their tale, a party was arranged.
But Mildred said, "I'll be right back. My outfit must be changed."

That night the party started. There was food and dancing too.
The Thornyclod brought some sweets that still tasted like glue.
They had a competition for the best dressed one of all.
  Mildred, they decided, was the "Belle" of the whole ball.

 And as the happy day was fading,
Swampy sat down with a friend.
What a lovely day it was," he smiled.
"But I'm glad it's now **THE END."**